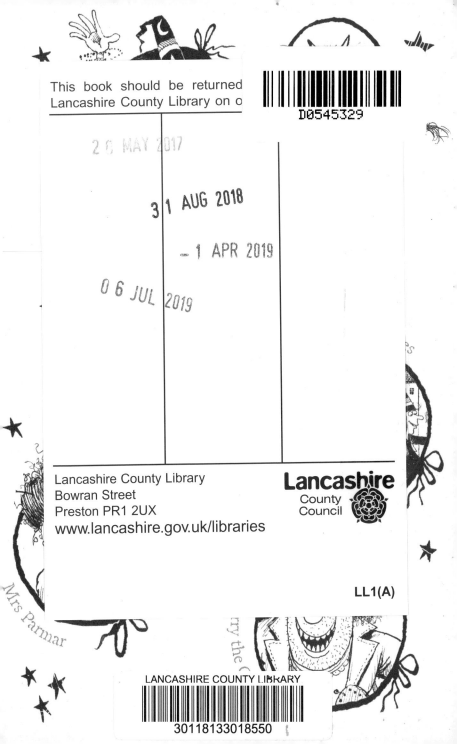

For Zara Brislin – K.P.
For Mick Goodhart with love – xx

OXFORD
UNIVERSITY PRESS

Great Clarendon Street, Oxford OX2 6DP

Oxford University Press is a department of the University of Oxford.
It furthers the University's objective of excellence in research, scholarship,
and education by publishing worldwide. Oxford is a registered trade mark of
Oxford University Press in the UK and in certain other countries

Text © Oxford University Press 2008
Illustrations © Korky Paul 2008
The characters in this work are the original creation of Valerie Thomas
who retains copyright in the characters.

The moral rights of the author/illustrator have been asserted

Database right Oxford University Press (maker)

First published in 2008
This edition first published in 2016

British Library Cataloguing in Publication Data
Data available

ISBN: 978-0-19-274832-4 (paperback)

2 4 6 8 10 9 7 5 3 1

Printed in Great Britain

Paper used in the production of this book is a natural,
recyclable product made from wood grown in sustainable forests.
The manufacturing process conforms to the environmental
regulations of the country of origin.

LAURA OWEN & KORKY PAUL

Winnie AND Wilbur

Whizz-Bang

WINNIE

OXFORD
UNIVERSITY PRESS

CONTENTS

Hot Cross WINNIE

7

WINNIE Gets Cracking

29

Broomstick
ALERT

53

Whizz-Bang
WINNIE

75

Hot Cross
WINNIE

Winnie's garden was as hot as a cauldron.
Wilbur lay under a rhubarb leaf with his
legs stretched and his tongue hanging out.
Along came Winnie wearing such dark
sunglasses that, **TRIP!**—

'Mrrrow!'

'Whoops! Blooming cat!' said Winnie,
rubbing her nose.

'Mrrow-ow-ow!' said Wilbur.

'Well, I'm hot too, you know!' said Winnie.

'I'm a hot cross witch and you're a hot
cross cat. We need to cool down.'

Winnie picked up the watering can and
watered her feet.

'Oo, that's nice!' she said, wiggling
her steaming toes. 'I wish, I wish . . .
Oo, I've got an idea!' said Winnie, and
she pointed her wand at the watering can.
'*Abracadabra!*' she shouted.

Instantly, there was a giant watering
can up in the sky, spilling down a great
showering waterfall of cold water.

'Lovely!' said Winnie, dancing in the
shower. 'Come on, Wilbur!' But Wilbur
was thrashing his wet tail and scowling
at Winnie. 'Whoopsy warts,' said Winnie.
'I forgot that cats don't like water!'

'Abracadabra!'

In another instant the watering can was gone. Winnie stood there, dripping and steaming.

'I'm sorry, Wilbur. Sorry, sorry, sorry. Now, can we be friends again?'

Wilbur closed his eyes.

'I'll magic you a sun hat. I'll magic you some sunglasses!' said Winnie. 'Abracadabra Abracadabra!'

Now Wilbur looked a dude, but he was still cross.

'This'll make you laugh!' said Winnie.
'What's brown and sticky and sounds like
a bell?'

Wilbur looked the other way and
pretended not to listen.

'Dung!' said Winnie. 'Dung's brown
and sticky and "dung" is the sound a big
bell makes! Get it?'

Wilbur just sniffed.

II

'I'll buy you a present, then. That'll cheer you up,' said Winnie. She got her broom.

'Jump up, Wilbur!'

Wilbur's ears flattened on his head, but he climbed on board.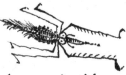

It was hot, flying.

'Let's go faster to make a breeze,' said Winnie. *Abracadabra!*

In an instant, Wilbur had to cling on to the broom with every claw. He lay flat and he closed his eyes, his tail whizzing out behind the broom.

'Wheeeee!' said Winnie. 'This is fun!'

'Mrrrow!' wailed Wilbur.

'Honestly! You just can't please some blooming cats!' said Winnie.

They got to the shops and parked the broom. But, 'Stop!' said Winnie. 'You wait in the broom basket, Wilbur, or you'll spoil your surprise.'

Wilbur was just climbing into the basket when a little girl called Clara noticed him.

'Hello, Pussykins!' said Clara. 'Are you hot, Pussykins? Are you hungry? Come with me!' Clara hauled Wilbur out of the basket. Wilbur was almost as big as Clara, but Clara managed to carry and drag Wilbur all the way to her house.

14

Clara's house was shady and cool.
Clara's fridge had cat food in it. Clara's
sisters all fussed over Wilbur and told him
what a very fine cat he was. Wilbur purred
so much that his whiskers sparked. Wilbur
was cool. Wilbur was being spoilt. Wilbur
was happy.

Winnie was feeling happier, too. As she
stepped into her favourite shop, a draught
of cool smelly air from a drain lifted her
hair and her dress and her spirits.

'Ooo!' giggled Winnie. 'This is lovely!'

Winnie looked at toad toasters and
mouse mincers and maggot mashers and
filth frothers and cockroach crushers and
bat broilers before she found what she was
after. She took her parcel back outside.

'Here I am, Wilbur!' said Winnie. 'Time
to go home.'

Winnie picked up her broom and gave
it a shake.

'Are you still sulking? Oh, stay in the
basket if you want to.' Winnie hung her
shopping from the front of the broom
and climbed on board.

'Ooooer!' said Winnie as the broom
tipped forwards because of the weight of
the parcel. 'You're heavy, Wilbur. And
you'll get even heavier after you've used

the present I've bought you. Can you

guess what it is?' asked Winnie as the

broom rose into the air.

Wilbur said nothing.

'You mardy old mog!' said Winnie.

'Don't you want to know?'

Still nothing.

Winnie was getting hot again. She

was getting cross too. So she didn't say

anything else to Wilbur all the way home.

Winnie parked her broom.

'We're home! Out you get!'

Winnie lifted the lid of the basket.

'WILBUR!' wailed Winnie . . . for the basket was empty.

Winnie felt empty too. Winnie felt desperate.

'Oh, my Wilbur, I've left you behind! Don't worry, Wilbur, I'm coming!'

Winnie jumped back onto her broom.

'*Abracadabra!*' she shouted.

Quick as a flash she shot through the
sky, back to the shops. Winnie looked
wildly all around.

'Where *is* he?' wailed Winnie.

'That black cat?' said a boy. 'Clara took
him.'

'What?' whispered Winnie. 'He's been
STOLEN?'

'They went that way,' said the boy.

Winnie waved her wand.

'**Abracadabra**, take me to Wilbur!'
begged Winnie.

In an instant Winnie was inside Clara's house, landing on Clara's dad's lap.

'A witch!' he yelped, and he leapt up, dropping Winnie to the floor. And suddenly Winnie was face to face with a grinning, drooling face that she knew and loved well.

'Oh, Wilbur!' said Winnie.

'He's going to live with me for ever and ever,' said Clara. 'Aren't you, Pussykins?'

Wilbur was purring and dribbling and working his claws as six small hands brushed him and put hair-clips in his fur.

'But he's *my* friend!' said Winnie. 'Look, I bought him a present!'

It was the little girls who ripped open the present and found . . .

'An ice-cream machine!' said Winnie.
'Do you like it, Wilbur? I thought we
could make maggot-flavour ice cream with
flea sprinklies to cool us down.'

But Clara's mum had other ideas. She
made strawberry ice cream with hundreds
and thousands on top. Clara and her sisters
were suddenly more interested in ice cream
than in cats.

'Quick, let's go home,' whispered
Winnie.

Without the ice-cream machine, the
broom was balanced just right. Winnie
and Wilbur flew at normal speed, calmly
over the countryside, and it was nice.

They landed in Winnie's garden.

'What shall we do now?' asked Winnie.

Wilbur grinned and pointed at the rhubarb patch. 'Prrrmeow,' he said.

'Good idea!' said Winnie.

Winnie and Wilbur lay under the shade of a big rhubarb leaf, watching the sun go down. Winnie held a stick with a bit of string tied to it with a centipede on the end which she waved up and down. As she flicked the centipede upwards, the toad on the leaf jumped for it, bouncing the leaf under him. So the leaf fanned Winnie and Wilbur till they were cool and comfortable and kind to each other again.

'I've got another joke for you,' said Winnie.

'Mrrow?'

'What's brown and sticky?'

Wilbur smiled. Wilbur pointed.

'Yes!' said Winnie. 'A stick is brown and sticky!'

WINNIE
Gets Cracking

When Winnie and Wilbur were queuing in the shop to buy their weekend sherbet bombs and gummy worms and liquorice rats' tails and pickled gherkins, they overheard Mrs Parmar, the school secretary, talking to the shopkeeper.

'I'll have a small box of cheap chocolates,' said Mrs Parmar.

'Special occasion, is it?' asked the shopkeeper.

'It's my birthday today,' said Mrs
Parmar. *Sniff!* 'Not that anyone takes any
notice of that. I can't afford much, but I
do buy myself a little bit of chocolate each
year. Nobody else will bother, and I do
love chocolate.'

'That's as sad as a soggy guinea pig with
no umbrella!' said Winnie, sticking her
large nose in between Mrs Parmar and the
shop man.

'Oh, it's you, is it, Winnie?' said Mrs
Parmar. 'I'm still trying to forget the times
you cooked and cleaned at the school!'
She clutched her box of chocolates and
backed away.

'Wilbur and me, we'll invite you for a birthday tea!' said Winnie. 'You come along to my house, Mrs Parmar, and we'll give you a real treat!'

A weak wobbly smile spread over Mrs Parmar's face. 'Well, I suppose that is kind of you, but . . .'

'See you at four, then,' said Winnie. 'And there'll be a present as well as lots to eat!'

'Food?' said Mrs Parmar, looking into Winnie's shopping basket. 'Oh, dear!' And she fled from the shop.

33

Winnie and Wilbur went home and
began to plan.

'What can we give her for a present?'
said Winnie. 'She's a smart lady. Would she
like some of that nice haggis hand cream?'

'Mrrro!' Wilbur shook his head.

'Well, what about a big black bar of
squashed slug soap?' Wilbur shook his

head even harder. 'No? Something pretty, then. What about a cowpat paperweight? Or maggot earrings? No? Or . . . or . . . I've got it!' Winnie clapped her hands in excitement. 'Remember that story about some thingy or other that lays a golden egg every day? Well, if we could get one of those for Mrs Parmar she would soon get rich! She could buy chocolate every day!'

Wilbur grinned his agreement.

'What exactly was it that laid the golden egg, Wilbur?' wondered Winnie. 'What came before the egg?'

Wilbur shrugged.

'Whatever laid the egg must have come out of an egg, mustn't it?' Winnie scratched her head. 'And whatever it was that laid *that* egg must have come out of another egg. And whatever . . . Oh, I know what! *Abracadabra!*'

In an instant the floor was rolling with eggs: big eggs, small eggs, speckled eggs, plain eggs, white eggs, pink eggs, rough eggs, smooth eggs.

'Keep them warm, Wilbur!' said Winnie. So Wilbur spread his furry warmth over as many of the eggs as he could, while Winnie crouched and hugged around the rest. It wasn't long before—

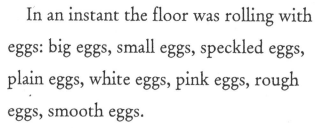

Crack!

'Whoops!'

Crack!

'Meeow!'

Crack-crack-crack!

—the eggs began to hatch. Out of this egg came that. Out of that egg came this. And out of the other eggs came those.

'Aren't they sweet? But I'd better grow them up fast, so that they can lay their eggs in time for tea. *Abracadabra!*' went Winnie.

And instantly the room was full of flapping and clucking and squawking and croaking and hissing. Then—**bump, splat! Crash, squish!** There were eggs being dropped all over the place.

'Can you see any golden ones, Wilbur?' asked Winnie. 'Oh, blooming rhubarb, what can we do with all these eggs?'

'Mrrow!' suggested Wilbur, miming eating with a knife and fork.

'Clever you, Wilbur!' said Winnie. 'We'll cook eggs for Mrs Parmar's birthday tea. Now, shoo all this lot out into the garden, will you, while I get cooking?'

With a hiss and a pounce, Wilbur soon had them all flapping and slithering and lumbering for the door and windows.

'Better get cracking!' said Winnie. She broke eggs and eggs and eggs and got whizzing with her mixer.

Winnie made woodlouse crunch soufflé. She made omelettes with toad tongue fillings. She made hard-boiled lizard egg and pondweed sandwiches.

'What a feast!' said Winnie. 'Set the table, Wilbur, it's nearly time. Put out proper napkins and everything because she's a very particular lady.'

42

Then Winnie stopped licking the mixing spoon as she remembered. 'Ooo, but we still haven't got her a present. And I *promised* her one! Oh, poor Mrs Parmar!'

'**Ding-dong!** Wiiiiinnnniiiieeee!' went the dooryell.

'It's her!'

43

Wilbur opened the door. There stood
a rather nervous looking Mrs Parmar in
her best dress.

'Come in!' said Winnie. 'Sit down!
We've made you a feast. There's even a
sponge cake with gherkin filling and lots
of candles. I wasn't sure how many
candles, so I just put on lots!' said Winnie.

'Oh!' said Mrs Parmar, looking at the table. 'I'm not *very* hungry, you know.'

'We might play some party games after, if you like!' said Winnie.

'I can't stay *very* long,' said Mrs Parmar, brushing some spiders off a chair and sitting down very carefully.

'Sandwich?' asked Winnie.

'Oh, those *do* look nice!' said Mrs Parmar in surprise. She took a sandwich and was about to bite into it when . . .

Clump-clump-clomp-plop!

A big brown creature walked across the table, lifted its tail, and laid an egg on the edge of Mrs Parmar's plate, catapulting the lizard egg and pondweed sandwich—**splat**—on to the far wall.

46

'Well, that *is* a surprise!' said Winnie, rather embarrassed. 'I'm ever so sorry, Mrs Parmar. I thought we'd got rid of all the hatchings before you arrived.' Winnie glared at Wilbur.

47

But Mrs Parmar had picked up the egg.
She looked at the egg. She sniffed the egg.
Then she nibbled the egg. And she smiled.

'Mrs Parmar?' said Winnie.

'This is wonderful!' said Mrs Parmar,
relaxing and laughing. 'I can't think of any
present I'd rather have than a freshly-laid
chocolate egg!'

'I did want you to have a golden one,'
said Winnie.

'But you can't eat golden eggs!' said
Mrs Parmar, taking another nibble.
Wilbur nodded his head to agree with
such wisdom, so rarely found
in people.

Mrs Parmar was too full of chocolate to eat anything else. But, once the tea was finished, they played 'Hunt the Chocolate Egg' because the chocodile had laid eggs all over the place.

'So many!' said Mrs Parmar. 'I can share them with the children at school. Then, perhaps, they might like me a little. That would be the best birthday present of all. Oh, thank you, Winnie!'

'You're welcome,' said Winnie. 'And you can take the chocodile as well, if you like.'

As she closed the door, Winnie said to Wilbur, 'Whoever would want chocolate, anyway, when they could have my trifle surprise?'

Broomstick
ALERT

'I'm bored!' said Winnie. 'I'm as bored as a snail is bored with the view inside its shell. I'm as bored as my toes are with the smell inside my socks. I'm as bored as . . .'

'Mrrow!' said Wilbur, and he put his paws over his ears.

'Am I being boring, Wilbur?' said Winnie.

'Mrrow!' said Wilbur crossly.

'What do people do to stop being bored?

Let's go down to the village and look in the library,' said Winnie.

The library was full of bookshelves, and full of people reading books.

'Look at them!' whispered Winnie. One person was laughing. Another looked frightened. 'How do books do that to people?' asked Winnie. She took a book from a shelf and looked at the black words on a white page that she couldn't read.

Those marks didn't make her cry or laugh or feel anything. Winnie turned the book the other way up, but it didn't make any difference. Wilbur was lying on the carpet with a book open in front of him and he was cat-laughing.

'Mrow-ha-ha!'

'I want to know what's funny!' said Winnie. 'I'm blooming well going back to that school!'

Winnie was in luck.

'Look at that, Wilbur! There's a whole flock of witches going to school today! And girls with plaits and stripy stockings and bears with suitcases and wizards with zigzags on their foreheads and . . . oh . . . almost everything except little ordinaries. They're as odd as a bag of ugly bug pick-n-mix. Come on, Wilbur, we'll fit in with the others today!'

'Who are you?' asked one small witch
in stripy tights.

'I'm Winnie the Witch,' said Winnie.

'So am I!' said the small one.

'Eh?' Winnie stood still and puzzled.
'How does that work, then?'

57

But Wilbur caught her cardigan in a claw and hurried her into the classroom.

The teacher, in a red cloak with a hood, was taking the register.

'Captain Teachum?'

'Here.'

'Professor Puffendorf?'

'Here.'

'Winnie the Witch?'

'Here,' said the little girl who had talked to Winnie earlier.

'Here,' said Winnie.

'Who are you?' asked the teacher, glaring at Winnie. 'And what is that cat doing in my classroom? We don't allow witches in school!'

'But—!' began Winnie, looking around at lots of witches. But the teacher was pointing at the door.

'Out!' said the teacher. So Winnie and Wilbur went out of the classroom . . .

Oooff! and walked straight into Mrs Parmar, the school secretary. She was looking flustered.

'Oh, Winnie, I'm desperate!' said Mrs Parmar. 'Today is our Book Day and the dog ate all the storyteller's books, so he's not coming, and I've got children waiting for stories and nobody to tell them unless . . . oh, Winnie, could you do it? Pleeeeease?'

A smile like the crack in a boiled egg grew across Winnie's face. 'Yes!' she said.

So Mrs Parmar led Winnie and Wilbur into the school library. Some children were sitting on the carpet, looking up at Winnie like vulture chicks in a nest waiting to be fed.

'Now, children,' said Mrs Parmar. 'Winnie here is going to read to you.'

'Read?' said Winnie. 'I—' But Mrs Parmar had already gone. 'Um,' said Winnie. She took a book from the shelf. 'Look,' she said. 'A picture of a lion!'

61

'Read the story!' shouted the little extraordinaries.

'I can't!' said Winnie.

Gasp! went all the little extraordinaries.

'But,' said Winnie. 'I can make stories come out of books another way.' Winnie waved her wand. *'Abracadabra!'*

Instantly there was a great big, growly, toothy, prowly lion right inside the room! It was licking its lips and sniffing children and opening its big pink mouth wide to swallow a—

'Abracadabra!' shouted Winnie, and
instantly the lion was gone. 'Phew!' said
Winnie, feeling as weak as a worm. 'Er . . .
wasn't that fun?'

'No!' said the little extraordinaries.

'Oh. I'll do you a better one,' said
Winnie. She picked up a book with a
picture of a rocket on the cover.
'Who'd like to go into space?'

'Me, me, me, me, me, me, me, me!!!'

shouted all the little extraordinaries.

'*Abracadabra!*' went Winnie.

65

And, instantly, there was a rocket in the room. The rocket was so big that it stuck right through the school ceiling and you could see the sky above it. Wind blustered in through the hole, making wings flutter and witchy hair whirl.

'Wow!' said the little extraordinaries, gazing up at the huge rocket.

And out of the rocket stepped a big robot spaceman.

Gasp! went the little extraordinaries.

'Fly with me to Mars,' commanded the robot. 'Together, we will fight the dreaded Xargottlenaughts!'

'Ooo, yes, let's all go to Mars!' said Winnie. 'Put on your spacesuits, everyone! Get on board.'

Winnie was hopping on one leg, trying to pull on her spacesuit. She didn't notice Wilbur sneaking out of the door. But suddenly the door burst wide open.

'WHAT ON EARTH IS GOING ON?' boomed Mrs Parmar.

'Oh!' giggled Winnie. 'It almost wasn't "what on earth", Mrs Parmar. It was almost "what on Mars"!'

Mrs Parmar inflated like a balloon. She pointed at the robot.

'You! Out! Cover your ears, children!'

They all crouched and covered their ears as the robot shut himself into his rocket and fired the engines.

ROAR!

WHOOOOOSH!

68

Up shot the rocket, leaving a great hole
in the library ceiling.

'Um, that's the end of the story.
The end,' said Winnie. So the hole closed
and everything went back to normal in the
library.

Mrs Parmar told the children, 'Out you

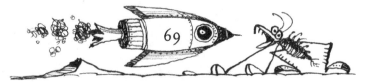

69

go and play.' Then she pointed at Winnie. 'You're fired!'

So Winnie and Wilbur went sadly out to the bike shed to collect the broom. They were just getting on board when there was a shout from the playground.

'Help!'

A gust of wind had caught the wings and capes of all the fairy and superhero little extraordinaries, and they were rising up into the sky and away from school!

'Help! Help!' they cried.

'I'm coming!' shouted Winnie.
'Hold tight, Wilbur!'

Up into the sky rose Winnie and
Wilbur on their broom. 'Grab hold
of Wilbur's paw!' Winnie told a fairy.
'Hold onto his tail!' she told a superhero.

And very soon Winnie had brought
them all safely back down to land.

'You saved the children, Winnie!'
said Mrs Parmar. 'You must come into
assembly so that the head teacher can
thank you properly.'

In assembly little Winnie the Witch
won the fancy dress prize. Big Winnie
the Witch won a medal for being a hero.

'You know what, Wilbur?' said Winnie as they walked happily home. 'There are more kinds of magic than *Abracadabra* magic.'

'Mrrow?' asked Wilbur.

'I think stories are magic too,' said Winnie.

'Purrrr,' agreed Wilbur.

Whizz-Bang
WINNIE

'Ooo, look at that! Fancy hanging your washing all over the street!' said Winnie as she and Wilbur flew over the village. 'Ooo, no! It's not knickers and socks, it's flags and bunting! There must be something going on in the village. Hold tight, Wilbur, let's go and find out what!'

They landed beside a man on a ladder, tying up the bunting. *Whoops!* He wobbled when he saw them.

'I didn't scare you, did I?' said Winnie. 'What's going on?'

'Big race, this afternoon,' said the man.

'What sort of a race?' asked Winnie.

'Proper one,' said the man, tying the last knot of the bunting string to the lamp post, and climbing down his ladder. 'Drivers in helmets and zip-up suits. Low down cars with big fat wheels that squeal and smoke when they go round corners.'

The man rubbed his hands together and smiled happily. 'It'll be a really proper race. Lots of noise. A few crashes. Tea afterwards.'

'What sort of noise?' asked Winnie.

'**Brrrrrrrrooooooom** sorts of noise!' said the man.

'Oh, I've got a broom!' said Winnie, waving her broom at the man.

The man laughed. 'That's a woman's kind of a broom, that is. That's a broom for cleaning, not for racing!'

'I could race you on this broom and beat you any day of the week!' said Winnie.

'Mrrow!' agreed Wilbur, flying a paw fast past the man's eyes to show him what Winnie's broom could do.

'Well,' said the man, 'if you take my advice, darling, you'll keep that broom in the kitchen and leave racing to the men and the machines.'

'Huh!' said Winnie. 'I'll see you this afternoon!'

The man shook his head. 'You can't go in for the race if your vehicle hasn't got wheels.' He pointed to a poster.

Hot wheels race! Open to all comers.

Sponsored by Tyres That Never Tire.

'No, love. You'd do best to help out with serving the teas. I'm sure the ladies could lend you a pinny.'

'I'll not be serving teas! I'll be serving you right, that's what I'll be serving!' said Winnie.

HOT
·WHEELS·RACE·
OPEN TO ALL COMERS!
Sponsored by
TYRES THAT NEVER TIRE

'Hadn't you better get back to hanging up your washing, mister? There's nothing to stop a broom having wheels, is there? Let's go on a wheel hunt.'

'Mrrow!' said Wilbur.

They looked in there. She looked under that. He looked inside those.

And they found wheels like this . . .

and this . . . and these . . . and those.

'Hand me the hammer, Wilbur,' said
Winnie. Then she began **bang-bang-
banging** the wheels onto her broom.

'There, Wilbur! Isn't that the best
wheelie broom you've ever seen? Hop on,
you can try it out, Wilbur!'

Wilbur's knees were knocking. Wilbur's ears were flat on his head.

'Put on your helmet.' Winnie rammed a bucket onto Wilbur's head.

'Hold tight!' said Winnie. Wilbur closed his eyes. He clung tight with his claws.

'Abracadabra!' shouted Winnie, waving her wand to make the broom go fast. Instantly rocket fire flared from the broom's bristles, and the broom shot

forward . . . and round in a circle. Round
and round and round and round so fast it
was just a blur of stick and twigs and fire
and frightened cat.

'Oh, botherarmarations!' said Winnie.
'We'll never win the race like that!'

'Mrrrrrroooooowwwww!' wailed
Wilbur.

'Oh, poor Wilbur!' said Winnie,
snatching up her wand. *Abracadabra!*

83

Instantly the broom stopped still.
But Wilbur didn't. He shot forward
and landed, with his head still spinning
round and round and round.

Winnie tried again. **Bang! Bang!
Bang!** 'Ouch, ouch ouch! Blooming
botherarmarations and fleas' fingernails,
I've banged my thumb!'

Winnie fixed the wheels again: this time
with bigger wheels at the back and smaller
wheels at the front.

'Hop on, we'll try again,' said Winnie.
'Mrrow!' Wilbur tried to run, but
Winnie caught him by the tail and plonked
him on the broom. 'Don't worry, I'm
coming with you this time! And I'm not
going to magic it fast.'

Winnie pulled the broom to the top of the hill. She sat on it, then pushed off . . . **whee-hup-bump-down—** 'Mrrow!'—**whee-hup-bump-down**—'Yeouch!'—**whee-hup—**

'Stop!' shouted Winnie, but the broom didn't stop. It went faster, and the **hup-bump** got faster too. 'Where's my wand?' screeched Winnie. '*Abra*—!' But Winnie's wand caught in one of the spokes of the wheels.

Lurch-skid-clatter-bang!

'Ouch!'

'Meowch!'

Bumped and bruised and banged and biffed, they got to their feet and looked at the scatter of wheels and the broken broom.

'We won't win any races on that!' said Winnie.

Just then they heard the loudspeakers down in the village announcing the race.

'It's about to start!' said Winnie. 'Come on, Wilbur! Even if we can't go in for the race, we can watch it! How are we going to get down there fast? I know . . . *Abracadabra!*'

In an instant, Winnie had roller skates on her feet. **Crash!** The next instant she'd fallen.

88

'Ouch!'

Holding on to Wilbur and rubbing her bottom, Winnie wobbled upright.

'You too, Wilbur!' she said.

'Abracadabra!'

Splat! Wilbur instantly had castors under each paw, and those castors had gone in different directions. Out went his legs. Down went Wilbur.

89

'Mrrow!'

'Come on, Wilbur! We're off!'

Winnie and Wilbur wobbled, then
strode, getting a little braver all the time.
Soon Winnie was bent over, one hand
behind her back, the other arm swinging
to speed her faster as she swished along
like a champion. There was a sound of
engines revving.

'Weeeeeee! Speeeeedy meeeee!' went
Winnie.

With a great roar, the cars were off and
racing!

'Come on, Wilbur!'

Wilbur copied Winnie's skating style
and managed to stay on his paws.

They got to the hill that ran down into the village just as the cars came around the corner.

'Weeeeee Ooooooo, Wilbuuuuuuurrr, this is a bit toooooo faaaaaast!'

'Mrrrow!' wailed Wilbur. Faster and faster they shot onto the road, whizzing past roaring cars. They were going a bit too fast.

92

'Wiiiillllllbbbbuuuurrrrr!' shouted Winnie. 'How do I make the skates stop?'

But Wilbur didn't know either. 'Mmmeeeeeeoooooowwwww!'

And suddenly both of them were tripped and tangled in tape.

'HOORAY!' shouted the crowd.

'Why are they cheering?' said Winnie. 'I've never had so many bruises in my life!'

93

'They're cheering because you won the race, missus!' said big Jerry from next door, stepping out of the crowd. 'Shall I carry you and Wilbur home?'

'That would be lovely,' said Winnie.
'I'll make us all a nice cup of garlic
blossom and ditchwater tea. Then it
will have been a proper race, with lots of
noise, a few crashes, and tea afterwards.'
'Lovely!' said Jerry.

Enjoy more magic moments with

Winnie AND Wilbur